The Holly Dog
Stories

- adventures of
a West London dog

*Best wishes.
Marjorie Evans +
Lyn Keay*

Stories by Marjorie Evans
Illustrations by Lyn Keay

TOWPATH BOOKS

Remembering

Bill and Dafydd

ISBN 978-0-9557558-0-4

TOWPATH BOOKS
37 Leyborne Park
Kew TW9 3HB

www.towpathbooks.co.uk

Printed and Bound in Great Britain by
www.printondemand-worldwide.com

WHO IS HOLLY?

Holly is one of those Spaniels who always looks untidy.

She has a curly black and white coat with a heart shape on her shoulder, soppy eyes, floppy ears and ploddy paws, and the softest, silliest look.

Daddy calls her N.T.B, Not Too Bright.

To all the family she is just 'Holly'.

1. HOLLY'S SWIM

Holly lives in Barnes with her family,
Mummy, Daddy, Alice and Jonny,

and quite a few things happen to her.

When Holly was
a young dog and hadn't
been out much on her own,
she longed to explore.

One day the family were all busy upstairs,

Mummy on the computer,
Daddy reading the paper,

Jonny drawing

and Alice
busy getting her doll
Marigold to sleep.

So...

Holly had her chance,

and no one noticed

when she ran out
of the front door
of number 96 Cleveland Road.

HOLLY WAS FREE!

It was a cold sunny
day, and Holly had a plan...

She walked down the road until she
came to Station Road.

She crossed carefully
and there it was...

BARNES POND

where she planned to have
a swim.

The ducks and swans looked at her doubtfully from the edge of the pond,

and one or two dogs walked obediently along the path with heads in the air.

It was just the day for a water dog to swim...

The ducks just ignored her as they were quite used
to silly dogs.

Holly gave a HUGE shake (for a small dog),
ran for the water...

and JUMPED!

What a SURPRISE!

She landed hard and instead of swimming, skidded to the far side of the pond.

If ever a duck
could laugh!

"Silly dog!
Didn't you know that water freezes
when it's cold, and you jumped
on to ICE?"

So much for her swim.

Holly wandered home VERY cold,
with VERY sore paws
and feeling VERY foolish.

2. THE REPUTATION

Holly was out and about with her friend Webster,
the Chocolate Labrador.

Holly was born in Oxfordshire so was a Country Dog.

She had also spent some time in the Army, so she was an Experienced Dog.

Webster was an Urban Dog and didn't know much about the country but still thought that he knew best.

He joined Holly in many of her adventures...

One day the dogs were with Alice and Jonny
having a marvellous time chasing kites in Richmond Park.
Webster had longer strides
but Holly had more speed.

It was wet and the
two children were
'puddling' in the
stream.

The dogs
loved the opportunity
to splash and muddy themselves too.

Suddenly a boy with a big yellow kite
came past.

Holly and Webster were
very excited
and tried
to grab it...

MISSED!

A mighty leap, but instead of catching the kite, Holly made a flying jump into the bracken.

She found herself looking up into...

...the angry eyes
of a very large brown animal
with the most ENORMOUS handlebars on his head.

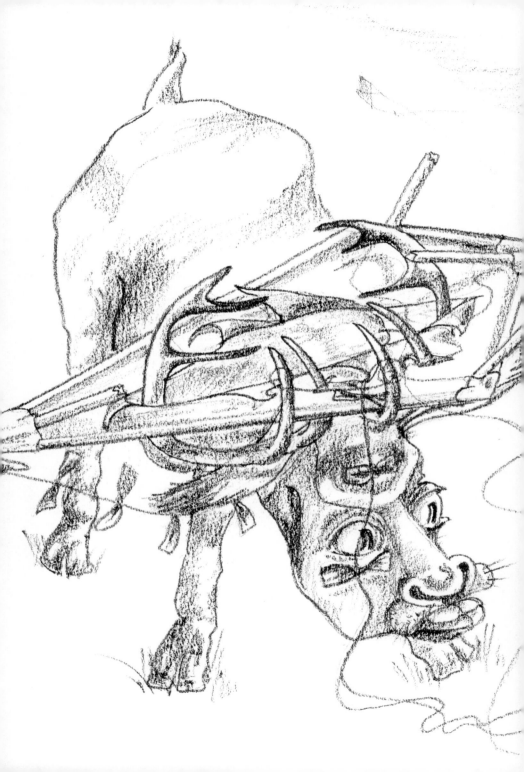

The yellow kite was caught on the
handlebars. Holly was very puzzled
and gave a friendly yelp.

The deer, for that is what it was, pushed his head down
and started to barge Holly.
"You don't mess around with animals like me," he said.

"I'VE GOT A REPUTATION."

Holly didn't know about Reputations,
but she knew that the deer needed help.

She and Webster pulled the kite away
with their teeth.

The deer was free!

The dogs barked, but the deer was still not too pleased, and looked angry.

The friends decided not to find out more about Reputations.

They turned tail and ran as fast as their legs would carry them.

Jonny and Alice
wondered why Holly and
Webster looked scared when
they emerged from the
bracken.

Webster made a mental note not to mess around with deer in Richmond Park in future.

Holly just wagged her tail and thought what fun it had been.

3. SECRET FRIENDS

Holly and Webster sneaked under the
iron turnstile.

No one saw the dogs because they were all looking
at a large fox who was wandering up the path

and stealing from the rubbish bin.

It was winter, cold and getting dark, and only a few people were left. No other animals seemed to be there at all

just two mischievous dogs.
Where were they?

At last they were in Kew Gardens.
They had heard all about it.

There were lots of lovely smells and they knew that it was fun because Alice and Jonny were always talking about their Climbing and Creeping there.

Someone shouted, "There's a badger!"

Someone else shouted, "There's a fox!"
But they weren't.

They were just two dogs out for a bit of fun.

There *were* other
animals there...

Two pairs of eyes
were watching
every move.

A black and white
striped head peeped out.

"You're not allowed in here," said Badger. "We're special
so we're allowed to stay, but we can always hide...
underground so most people
never see us."

From the dark bushes, a small, shy animal with a dark,
glossy coat appeared.
Mole said, "We're the Secret Animals of Kew."

Round the Lake, over the Shiny Bridge, into the woods, past the Waterlily Pond and round the Pagoda...

RIVER THAMES

LAKE

SHINY BRIDGE

Off went Holly and Webster
with their new friends.

Which way did
they go?

Webster saw some green spotted newts
lazing by the Lake,

and Holly saw a bright
green parakeet in a tree.

"Keep away! Keep away!" he screeched.
"They are looking for you. I can fly
so they never catch me."

The friends were having a marvellous time
chasing birds and squirrels,

but definitely didn't want to be caught.

"Hide in my sett," said Badger, but they were too big to get in.

They could hear heavy boots in the undergrowth coming closer and closer…

"Quick, quick, this way!
Fox has made a bigger hole under the gate by the river."

Holly and Webster wriggled through.

They were out at last!

"See you soon," called their
Secret Friends.

It was a long way home, and they were very weary, but now they knew of the Secret Animals of Kew.

Not even Alice or Jonny knew about this adventure.

THE END